This edition published by Parragon Books Ltd in 2017
and distributed by

Parragon Inc.
440 Park Avenue South, 13th Floor
New York, NY 10016
www.parragon.com

ISBN 978-1-4748-4502-1

T#489514

Printed in China

Marshall Saves the Day!

PaRragon

Bath · New York · Cologne · Melbourne · Delhi
Hong Kong · Shenzhen · Singapore

Marshall had been doing exercises in front of the Lookout all week. He was training for the Fastest Fire Pup trophy!

"Hose out!" barked Marshall, taking aim. He shot water from the hose and straight into a bucket. "I did it!"

The other pups cheered him on.

Next, Marshall had to perform a rescue. He drove his fire truck to a tree where Cali the cat waited.

But the ladder hit the tree and broke, and Marshall fell with a *BUMP!*

I'm okay!

Ryder watched from the Lookout.
"It looks like Marshall could use a helping hand,"
he said, pushing a button on the PupPad.

"PAW Patrol
to the Lookout!"
With that, all the
Pup Tags lit up,
and then the team
raced to the tower.

In the control room, the pups lined up, ready for action.
"This time, Marshall is the emergency. He needs our help,"
said Ryder. "But we just want you to do your best and not
worry about whether you break the record."
"Do my best and forget the rest," said Marshall.

"Rocky, I need you to find something in your recycling truck to fix Marshall's ladder," said Ryder.

"Don't lose it, reuse it!" Rocky said.

The pups raced out of the Lookout.

Outside, Rocky rummaged in his truck,
looking for something to fix the ladder.

Rocky
to the
rescue!

"This broom will work," barked Rocky. "I'll use the handle to make new rungs for your fire ladder, Marshall."

Rocky screwed the new rungs into place.

Ryder received a call. It was Mayor Goodway! "There's a TV crew waiting to film Marshall break the Fastest Fire Pup record," she said. "He's late!"

I'm fired up!

"Marshall's ready to go," Ryder assured the mayor.

Let's roll!

The PAW Patrol had to get Marshall
to the starting line right away.

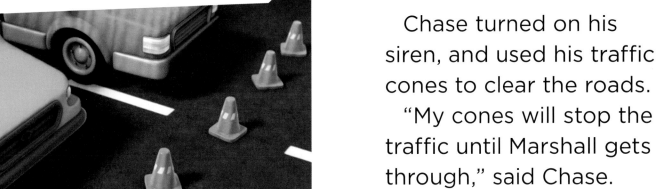

Chase turned on his siren, and used his traffic cones to clear the roads. "My cones will stop the traffic until Marshall gets through," said Chase.

As soon as Marshall
arrived at the park,
the TV crew turned
on their cameras.

"You're on in three . . .
two . . . one. . . ." said
the cameraman.

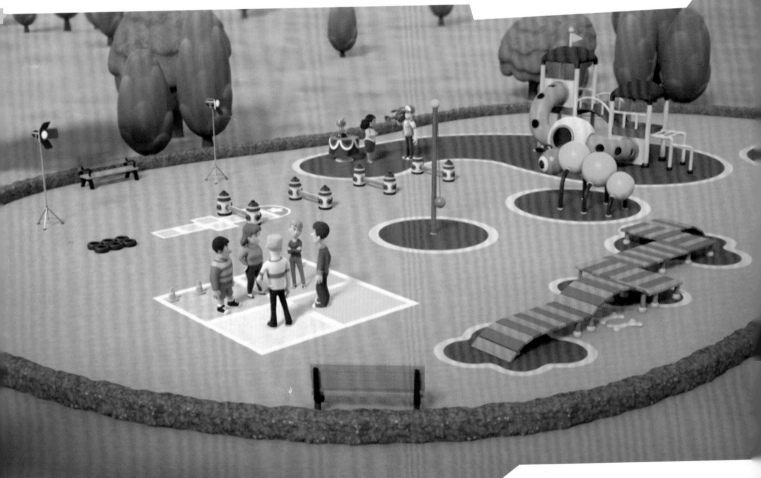

"Today, Marshall the Fire Pup will attempt to win the trophy for completing the Fire Rescue Course in the fastest time ever," said Mayor Goodway.

The crowd went wild!

"If Marshall can ring the City Hall bell in less than 10 minutes," the mayor continued, "he'll be the Fastest Fire Pup ever! Go!"

Marshall started the race. "Do my best and forget the rest!" he said to himself.

First, he completed the obstacle course. Then, he used his ladder. With the new rungs, Marshall easily climbed up, and rescued the toy cat from the tree.

Marshall raced his fire truck to the beach to complete the next task. "Hose out!" barked Marshall, as he took aim.

A stream of water put out a fake campfire. Everyone cheered!

"I did it!" said Marshall. "Now I just have to get to City Hall and ring the bell."

But just as Marshall was about to get into his truck, he spotted a fire . . . a *real* fire!
"I'll take care of that!" barked Marshall. "Hose out!"
Marshall put out the fire with his Pup Pack hose. Hooray!

Everyone cheered for Marshall—especially the mayor!

"You've got 30 seconds left," said Ryder. "Give it your best!"

Marshall zoomed to City Hall, raced up his ladder to the bell tower, and rang the bell.
BONG!
But he was one minute too late! Marshall wasn't the Fastest Fire Pup.

But Mayor Goodway was proud of him.
"You stopped to put out a *real* fire and that
makes you an Adventure Bay hero!"

She presented Marshall with the trophy.
"This trophy is now . . ." she said, "for the
Greatest Fire Pup in the World!"

And everyone cheered!

Later, back at the Lookout, the PAW Patrol watched Marshall on the news.

"You did it, Marshall!" the pups barked.

"I really did do my best!" he said.

The End